Air & other Stories

Lauren Leja

Nixes Mate Books
Allston, Massachusetts

Book design by d'Entremont
Cover photograph by Lauren Leja

Some of these stories appeared in *5x5 Singles Club*, *Primal Primer*, and *Nixes Mate Review*

Of course, a gigantic thank you to Michael McInnis. With gratitude to Lisa Carver, Gary Lutz and Michael Martone. And with endless appreciation for the perpetual support of Natalie Curley, Jim Linderman, Rick Moody and Anne Russo.

ISBN 978-0-692-90374-2

Nixes Mate Books
POBox 1179
Allston, MA 02134
nixesmate.pub/books

Today

Oh! kangaroos, sequins, chocolate sodas!
You really are beautiful! Pearls,
harmonicas, jujubes, aspirins! all
the stuff they've always talked about

still makes a poem a surprise!
These things are with us every day
even on beachheads and biers. They
do have meaning. They're strong as rocks.

— Frank O'Hara, *The Collected Poems of Frank O'Hara*

Contents

Tan   1

Hands   14

Fanta   27

Haircut   30

Air   37

Air & other Stories

TAN

WE WERE JEALOUS of Brenda and went over her house whenever we could. Brenda had a trampoline in the backyard and pinball machines, airhockey, bumperpool and a tanning lamp in her basement rec room.

Brenda's parents were divorced and the three girls, Brenda, BB and Bonnie lived with Mom, and her two brothers Jason and Jeff lived with Dad. Dad, partly because he felt guilty and partly because he was an asshole, kept buying the girls anything and everything they wanted – it was like living in a game show. Brenda's father answered the phone once – that was during the divorce – and his voice sounded mad and tired. He called Brenda to the phone then let it drop to the floor.

I never met her Mom – she was always "out." I never knew exactly what that meant – none of us did and no one wanted to be the one to ask. But Linda, Brenda's Mom, did exist – her photos followed you up the hall stairs. Linda in a crochet bikini, Linda wearing a tight pink "Yes, I'm STILL 29" tshirt perched on the hood of her Beetle, waving at the camera with one hand and fluffing her permed halo with the other. I didn't know much about Linda except that she let the girls do pretty much whatever they wanted without burning the house down. I think that after the divorce, when she gave up yelling at us girls, was the beginning of the end. We all went nuts. The basement became our refuge; soon it started to look like a suburban version of the Playboy mansion, but instead of the Bunnies, there was just us, the handful of stoned and drunk teenage girls in tanktops, stupidly trying to play airhockey with the table unplugged.

The bus dropped me off at the end of Brenda's street and I clomped down the two blocks, cool in my clogs, to number 34. The house was kind of ugly – a dirty orange two-story with brown shutters plopped in the middle of a dry, dead summerlawn, a giant forgotten jackolantern. The green hose with attached sprinkler snaked over the sad grass leaving rotted zigzags and tiny birds flapped in the dirtbaths that pitted the yard. I clomped down the gravel sidewalk next to the garage, slid open the sliding glass door and stepped through the smoky heavy curtains in the living room. Brenda's house was dark; it was always dark and cool. It was like walking into a movie theatre in the middle of the show: you needed to sit a minute to let your eyes adjust.

I dragged out a barstool and had a cigarette, watching the smoke feather out in the air. I blew smoke rings at the macrame owl wallhanging, aiming at the big bead eyes. When the furniture stopped being shadows and became furniture again, I opened the fridge and the white triangle of refrigerator light blinded me as I grabbed the tupperware jug of cherry KoolAid and vodka, found my favorite loopy crazy straw and headed into the basement for my weekly tanning session.

. . .

I MET BRENDA through her sister BB, my driver's ed instructor. BB was the cool big sister everybody wished they had. BB never graduated highschool — she had been kicked out too many times for smoking pot in the handicapped bathroom — but her boyfriend Tim's father owned the driving school and felt bad for her and being a twelve-stepper himself, gave her the job. The weird thing was that Tim's father wouldn't give Tim a job and he had to drive the potato chip truck, filling up the vending machines at the airport and the hospital. Tim's father thought it would teach Tim to be more responsible if he had a job where he wore a uniform and besides, there was no way he would ever get the chance to smash up one of the special driving school cars.

I met BB for eight Friday afternoon driving sessions. That first time the big yellow car pulled up alongside my mailbox, horn blaring. Far away from my front porch, I could see only see the orangy smudge of the driver struggling to slide into the passenger seat. I was afraid of the car, afraid of hitting some kid on a Bigwheel, afraid of making myself a quadriplegic. The smudge screamed "Let's get the hell out of here!" The smudge pumped an arm out the window: "Ka Ren, Ka Ren! Let's go!"

Slowly I staggered down the driveway, toward the beckoning hand, the fingers flashing silver, thumbs and pointers.

"Hey, get in the F-ing car! Are you nervous? You look nervous! Don't be nervous. Look – there's an extra brake on my side if you fuck up!"

I stuck my head in the driver's window. The first thing I saw was hair – a huge puddle of bright orange hair, as scary orange as orange crush, everywhere. BB's eyes were like tiny spiders, too much Maybelline making the furry little legs. She was wearing what I soon realized was her uniform – a tight leather vest and cut off jean hot shorts over suntan pantyhose. The too-dark equator of the control top circled a few inches beneath the white fringed hem of the shorts.

BB smiled her chapstick smile and I slid behind the wheel.

She accordioned her feet up onto the dash, clogs crunching the plastic. The long metal bar poked through both sides of the carpeted island of Tab cans and lipstick tissues and sticky candy wrappers, twin pedals on each side. "Karen, don't think so much, just do it. I can stop if something happens." The suntan of her legs sparkled like shiny sausages.

I stopped worrying and started to drive.

Lessons 1, 2, and 3 we drove around the parking lot at the KMart, looping around the big lettered signs and sometimes we went to The Mall parking garage where I drove the never-ending spiral to the roof and coasted down the rollercoaster exit ramps. Lessons 4, 5, 6, and 7 were the fun ones, the ones all the girls had told me about. I drove to the Drive-Thru at the bank where BB would space out and throw the plastic tube into the backseat, to the Dairy Queen, and to the grubby hippy's house to pick up suspicious paper shopping bags, and always last to the QwikSavMart to visit her sister Brenda who worked the register. BB would hand me her folded over shopping list while she chainsmoked and fiddled with the eight track.

BB's cigarette was like her eleventh finger. Brenda had worked at the QwikSavMart for a year and was used to being BB's slave and feeder. I met Brenda when I handed her the list.

"So you're the latest favorite. Are you Karen?" Brenda asked me.

I nodded "Yeah, I guess so."

Brenda wore long feather earrings and a stiff labcoat with QwikSavMart stitched over her heart. Her mouth was like a coloring book, the bright red bleeding outside the lines of her skinny lips. She had BB's wild hair.

"I've still got another half hour to drive today. Can I just get BB's stuff and go?"

Brenda shook her fluffy head no. "It'll take a while—this list is tricky. See, BB doesn't give me a real list. She just writes down a color and I have to fill up a bag with food that's that color or at least the wrapper is. Red and green are pretty easy, but pink and grey are hard as hell. Thank god the cigarettes are always the same. Want a Slurpee while you wait? Blueberry Blast or Raspberry Riot?"

I slurped while Brenda walked the aisles, filling the shopping bag. Today's color was orange. Doritos, tangerines, a six pack of Orange Crush, carrots, Kraft macaroni and cheese, Fruity Pebbles, Reese's peanut butter cups, melting Creamicles, Cheezwhiz, fishsticks, a Starburst family pack and Tang.

"Here's the stuff. Good luck on your driving test."

Two weeks later I barely passed my driving test and started to visit Brenda at the QwikSavMart, always walking or taking the bus. Without BB around with the second brake, I was terrified to be in a normal car. Of course I told everybody that my mother was a bitch and wouldn't let me use her deathmobile.

BB moved on to her next batch of impressionable and paying teens and I, the orphan, visited Brenda at QwikSavMart. I sat on a milkcarton behind the counter, smoking shitty generic cigarettes, the only brand the owner didn't bother to count every night. Brenda only let us steal the stuff that couldn't be traced – Slurpees, cheese dogs, Bazooka, fountain drinks and that scary unnaturally yellow radioactive popcorn – or was out of sight of the video surveillance cameras. I think her job at QwikSavMart made her feel important, the only place where people listened to her – she was the Queen. Brenda controlled the gas pumps with a flip of the switch and decided which underage kids got to buy beer and which got their fake IDs scotchtaped to the cashregister. She was responsible for making the coffee, filling the hot dog merry-go-round, rotating the milk, and restocking the candy and the car magazines. The only thing she refused to do was clean the bathrooms. Brenda twirled the bathroom key baton over her head and chanted, "I don't clean 'em at home I don't clean 'em here." By that time I had been to her house and knew this to be true.

We hung out most nights at the QwikSavMart until Brenda's shift was over. We took turns imitating the crazy guy who hung out at the video games muttering under his breath "Tits...tits" to every person, male or female, who passed by. We smoked and drank giant cups of Tab and carefully slid the cheap porno mags out of their plastic wrappers and read the cheesy letters aloud over the gas microphone, half laughing and half amazed. We made fun of all the retarded customers and complained about school, our fucked up families and boys and argued about tv shows and makeup and rockstars.

We became best friends.

• • •

I HEADED DOWN into the basement for my weekly tanning session. Brenda wouldn't be home until eleven when her shift ended, so I could chill out, catch a much needed buzz, and listen to some tunes.

The far corner of the basement was the beauty corner. Knots of cords from the curling iron and blow dryer and electric comb tangled under the tv tray packed with shoe boxes of cheap stolen makeup and barrettes. Slippery piles of hairstyle magazines and wordfind books slid over the floor. Brenda and I spent a whole weekend stapling long rolls of QwikSavMart tinfoil to the ceiling, two walls and floor to construct our tanning salon and ensure our even baking. Even BB had come downstairs to inspect our masterpiece: "Pretty fuckin' cool, you guys."

I suction the straw and watch the red spiral up the loops in stripes. I put Aerosmith on the stereo and clamp on the puffy headphone earmuffs. Off comes my clogs, shirt and bra. I peel and wriggle out of my tight corduroys and smear the slick baby oil across my body, shiny and warm.

Steven Tyler screams into my ears and I dance under the dangling tanning lamp hanging from the ceiling, I dance to my fake sun on a string in the corner of a dark basement covered in tin foil. The curly umbilical cord to the headphones keeps me in the proper orbit. I wiggle and grind and sweat my way through side one. I watch myself in the silver funhouse, a wrinkly blur surrounded by patches of light. I practice my Soul Train moves, trying to do what the girls on tv do and quickly realize that I am a shitty dancer and am glad that I have no witnesses. The voices and the KoolAid and the too hot heat are all mixed up inside me, dripping into my brain, and I feel dizzy and hot and confused. I need to lay down.

I drag over the saggy pool chair covered with a Budweiser towel and plop down and adjust the pink strings and triangle of my tuesday panties and I adjust my socks. I fumble for the tiny eightsided box of paper cupcake holders jammed into the plastic cupholder screwed to the chair and crown my nips – pink on the left, yellow on the right. It is important to tan safely.

Another long suck on the crazy straw and I am on my way to a boozy coma. Inside my real tight eyes spindly stars and dandelions and fireworks float in the electric black.

Bass pounds in my ears; my earrings vibrate.

...I'm lying by the pool in Los Angeles in my gold bikini waiting for my agent to call and my very close personal friend Steven is serenading me...

Suddenly an eclipse.

I can feel the shadow over me and open my eyes.

The eclipse is a tall guy leaning into my sun. "Hey, you drank all my KoolAid."

It's BB and Brenda's face on a guy and the hair's the same and so is the leather vest.

"You drank all my KoolAid," he repeats, "and you have no shirt on."

Pointing out my nakedness makes me panic but I tried to be cool as I mummified myself in the Budweiser towel. "I'm tanning. Are you one of the hologram brothers? I never thought you existed in real life."

"Yeah, I'm Jason."

"I'm Karen. I'm waiting to meet Brenda, so relax about the stupid KoolAid. Brenda can always steal more."

"You know, when I was little, I used to fill my mouth with KoolAid powder and chugalug from the hose and chase Brenda and BB around the yard, spitting at them. My Mom was pissed because I turned all their tshirts into tiedye."

"Brenda never mentioned cherry and grape spit." I tugged on my towel. "Turn around so I can get dressed." I frantically searched for my stuff and pulled it on as fast as I could, everything sticking to the baby oil in a really gross way. My corduroys were soggy. "The best thing we used to do was run down the street late at night and throw tennis balls at the bats flying around. We never hit any but they made these cool screeching sounds because they have this radar thing and then my Mom would yell at us and say that the bats would bite us and give us all rabies."

At the sound of my zipper Jason spun around. "Want to go for a ride? Then maybe we can pick up Brenda."

"I guess so," I said, and shut down my tanning salon. "Let's go."

Why was I going with a wildhaired stranger in a leather vest who I just met while I was shiny and naked in his cellar and who was the foxy brother of both the girl I idolized and my best friend? I went because it seemed like it was going to be okay.

Out in the driveway I looked around for a car but there was just a giant dirty ambulance. "Where's the car, Jason?"

"Man, I feel like a loser." He pushed a stringy strand of hair behind his ear, the spider ring on his pointer and the skull ring on his thumb clinking. "My car's fucked up so the guys at work let me borrow this but I had to promise not to use the siren."

"You work at the hospital?" I didn't like to think about sick and old people's germs. My tshirt was plastered to my back and I felt the slow creeping of a wedgie in progress.

"I work in the emergency room cleaning up the puke and changing the tv channels so there's no fights and stuff like that, but I'm really taking nightclasses to be an EMT."

"I've never been in an ambulance before. I think I need some Lysol – this germ thing bums me out."

"Karen, try to think of this as my van and besides, the germs are too old to do anything anyway. Get in."

We hop in and the doors close with a heavy thud. My seat is high up and I like that. Jason stretched his arm behind my seat as he backed out of the driveway, his long blue sleeves carefully rolled up above his elbows, very flat and tight. He smells like cigarettes and ketchup and disinfectant. We zoom down the by now dark street. "I think we need to get a little high."

Jason steers with his knees while groping through the glove compartment, pulling out the bulging prize bag and wedging the plastic baggie between his denim thighs. He shakes out some pot and rolls it on a white square of tissue paper that has magically appeared, automatic and fluid. His tongue flicks and licks as he guides the ambulance with his knees. As we take a really fast curve there's the hollow metallic scraping of a runaway oxygen tank rolling around in the back. Left right left straight. He twists one end of the tube shut and pinches it and then the other and jabs the joint between his lips. His right hand steers while the left pats his pockets – jeans, shirt, vest. "Where's my lighter?"

I find some matches in the crack of the seat. "Let me do it." Jason turns his face towards me and the match lights up his face in yellow light for a second, then dies with a drift of sulphur. His eyes are green like a cat and they close as his lips suck, greedy, on the joint, holds it and then exhales. The air smells sweet. We pass the joint back and forth, quietly smoking, and I take off my clogs, feet on the dashboard, hugging my knees. It is almost too quiet. There is no radio in an ambulance.

Our headlights illuminate the black road, slicing it into thick chunks of light, narrow tunnels between the trees and I watch Jason's hands shift on the steering wheel from six-thirty to quarter-of-three, thumbs hooked onto the inside spindle.

Suddenly Jason shuts off the headlights and we head down the dark crooked backroad to the airport, the supersonic vaccuumcleaner sounds of the planes are closer and overhead and I feel like we are zooming down a treelined rollercoaster up and around, down down down then up. Jason isn't driving really fast but the darkness and the pot are speeding everything up. And at every curve I swore we would crash into a wall of blackness that swung out suddenly like a gate from among the trees.

HANDS

BRENDA AND I LOVE to watch the retards through the windows. There's this stubby building a few blocks away from the high school and it's called Work, Inc. and the retards and crazies work there. Brenda and I drag the mangled milk crate up the fire escape of the next door HairHutt and share a smoke and watch the retards work.

We first noticed the place this summer when the Work, Inc. van dropped off in front of the building.

"WORK, INC: WE HELP THE DISABLED BECOME ABLE", was painted in rainbow letters on the van doors. When the van stopped, flashing lights went on. CAUTION: CHILDREN CROSSING.

Brenda squealed and pointed: "Children my ass! Look – they're all too old!"

We were expecting a couple of kids in wheelchairs or maybe on crutches. Jesus, even a blind kid. But they were all pretty old, some twenty, some thirty, and a few teenagers, and they all seemed a little fucked up. They lurched and jerked out of the van like mini-Frankensteins.

A few had really big heads and little bodies. A girl with red hair was drooling, the spit in little webs from her chin to her chest. She wore a bib. A short fat guy in brown polyester pants with suspenders was dragging a giant rubber snake in the gutter, through the dead leaves and losing scratch tickets and Burger King wrappers that flew up like butterflies as he passed. A wiry looking kid with scratches all over his arms wore a hockey helmet covered with Muppet stickers and he was rocking back and forth. And hopping out of the other side of the van was a really hot guy with a black wispy mustache and long hair. He wore a faded KISS baseball shirt.

"Shit, he's foxy!" Brenda whispered. "He must be the driver – he's the only one who doesn't have a giant Mr. Potato Head head."

I had to admit that I was checking him out too.

Then a frazzled black lady in a pink smock zoomed around with a clipboard, herding the Work, Inc.-ers closer to the van. Her giant gold earrings tinkled like Christmas ornaments. "Okay you kids – I need to count you all to make sure nobody snuck out of the van. Frank, Frank, hey I see you!"

Mr. Plastic Snake smiled and whipped his pet around his head with a big whoosh.

"Okay, I see that Julie is here."

The drooling redhead girl was lying on the sidewalk. She wasn't going anywhere.

"Julie, please wake up. Thomas? Thomas?"

A crew cut guy with Mickey Mouse glasses waved his hand in the air without interrupting his quiet chant: "5 times 4 equals 20, 5 times 5 equals 25, 5 times 6 equals 30, 5 times 7 equals 35..."

The lady called out "Alan", and saluted Hockey Helmet and checked off her clipboard. "And Rob, Rob, are you with us today?"

Our hottie answered, "Hey Marcia, I'm cool", and waved. He had no hands.

Brenda and I freaked.

Instead of hands there were little bumpy knobs at the end of his wrists like tiny play-dough fingers that had never been stretched out.

"Shit, I never thought I'd think a guy with no hands was sexy. Man, I didn't know. Hey, Karen, swear you won't tell anyone, okay?"

"Who could I tell? I thought he was way sexy too!" I told her.

And that was the day my obsession with Rob began.

• • •

ALL DAY in summer school I kept thinking about Work, Inc. and Rob. Behind my fanned geometry book I retraced RobRobRob with my see-thru rainbow pen in red, blue, and green. Why was he at Work, Inc.? What did he do there all day? Was he retarded too or was it just the hand thing? Was he born without hands or was it from a snowblower accident? Was his family normal? What was Rob's favorite tv show? How did he eat? Gloves or mittens or the dangling sleeve in the winter? Did he wear a watch? Could he ride a bicycle? How did he pee? Did he like to get high?

The teacher's voice droned and drifted: "Parallelogram, trapezoid, rhombus, equilateral triangle... measure off 60 degrees from the center with your compass..."

I imagined myself combing Rob's long hair and feeding him Doritos one by one while we watched The Night Stalker. Rob would kiss me during the Stridex commercials and I would smear cherry chapstick all over his lips and we would be very happy.

• • •

BRENDA AND I went to the fire escape practically everyday and she brought her Mom's binoculars and we started to figure out what went on at Work, Inc., the rhythms of the day. The main thing we realized was that everything took much longer for them than for regular people. Just putting away their lunchboxes and taking off their coats could last an hour. Some couldn't unbutton themselves. Some couldn't stop buttoning and unbuttoning, like firemen in a time drill. Some just stood there helplessly, forgetting what they were supposed to be doing in the first place. We stopped seeing the big picture and noticed the details even more: the chin hairs, the Ronald McDonald striped socks, the soggy candy necklaces staining chubby necks. Karen said she kept going because the Work, Inc. people made her feel better about herself and she liked to spy and we were the only ones from the high school cool enough to do it. I was too afraid to confess my crush and claimed to be doing research for the next science fair.

As far as we could tell, the Work, Inc.-ers did the shitty jobs that no one else would do. How were they going to be picky and say no? We chainsmoked and watched from the HairHutt fire escape as the workers tested Christmas tree bulbs in July. They each had a long board with six sockets on it. They had to screw in six bulbs at a time, flip the switch and see which bulbs were burnt out. Then they had to throw the lousy bulbs into a "Bad" box (with a magic marker sad face on it) and put the others into a "Good" box (smiley face).

No one could seem to get a handle on it. Frank-the-Snake kept stuffing the bulbs into the snake's mouth; the snake soon looked like it had swallowed a rabbit. The Chanter was great at screwing and unscrewing all the bulbs into the board but couldn't get much further than that. Julie-the-Drooler seemed like the only one who could master the complexities of the project even if it did take her an hour to go through twenty four bulbs. She chomped down on her fleshy tongue and squinted in cartoon concentration as she worked.

Operation Light Bulb lasted almost a month. Even though we were both fascinated – the total slow motion underwaterness of it all, the very real confusion – sometimes we just had to escape to save our own already shaky mental health. Brenda would take a Sun In break and squirt our heads with the sticky goo and I would do a puzzle from my Word Find book and we'd run off to Brenda's house for a box of Jax Snax. And when we'd start watching again it was like we'd never left. Work, Inc. was like our own private family reunion and we were always the success stories.

I think it was between the popsicle project ("Please make a bundle of ten (10) popsicle sticks and secure them tightly with two (2) rubber bands") and the soap bags ("Please insert one (1) miniature Irish Spring Deodorant Soap Bar into plastic bag; Next, please insert one (1) 15–cent off coupon") that the binoculars and I figured out what Rob did at Work, Inc. He was not at the long tables with the others and the piles of popsicle sticks and tiny green soaps. Standing on the milk crate, I could see in a corner, near the Sad–Kitten–Doing–A–Pullup poster (Hang in There!), an easel and paints and family size cans of brushes and some scuzzy rags and a radio and an avocado green corduroy Lazy Boy recliner.

Rob's hair was pulled back in a low ponytail and he was painting with a long brush in his mouth like those cigarette holders in old fashioned movies. There was a ripped out page from National Geographic clamped to the easel and Rob was slowly copying its bald eagle flying over the snowy mountaintops. Except in Rob's version, the eagle was blue and purple and shooting out of the flames and oozing lava of a stumpy little volcano floating in the middle of a foamy green ocean. My Rob was an artist and artists are different than the rest of us – they don't have to explain things – they just have to make stuff.

I watched with the binoculars until I got a headache from squinting. Rob painted very slowly. Every few minutes he put down his brush and sipped MelloYello through a crazy straw and stared at his project or tried to push back falling hair with a tiny hand. He never seemed satisfied, adding more fire, more lava, a few rockets. Brenda reminded me that the binoculars were hers and that she needed to check out Rob's amazing mouth action for herself. I told her she wouldn't understand but handed over the binoculars. While Brenda was spying, I put my magic marker in my mouth and tried to write my name on the cover of the puzzle book. It was impossible and the slimy marker kept sliding out and I felt like Julie-the-Drooler and I realized that Rob must truly be a master.

Rob's painting changed everything – we would live in the mountains and I'd set out his MelloYello and his paints and I would feel like Audubon's wife, and prop up the dead birds in plastic branches and styrofoam rocks and fill their beaks with gummy worms. Rob would be famous and sell his mouth paintings to museums and rich game show hosts and senile kings of faraway countries.

• • •

ON SUNDAY I went to the Mall to meet Brenda and spend the money my mom gave me for school clothes. I got an Orange Julius from the Food Court and glided and slurped up the escalator to look for Brenda at the caboose shaped TShirt Xpress. I saw a strange flash of pink and turned. Sprawled on the ground in front of the

Stairway to Heaven Headshop was Julie-the-Drooler, twisting the straps of her plastic bag tightly, so tightly the bag unwinds really fast like a small pink helicopter over her head. She smiles and with her red hair and orange sweatshirt she looks like a giant cotton candy explosion.

"Julie, are you okay?" I asked, actually talking to her for the first time though I had been spying on her for two months.

"Jean, my name is Jean. Jean Nate, just like the yellow lady on the television." She smiled and patted the wrinkled pink bag. A snail's trail of drool oozed from the corner of her mouth.

"Ok, Jean, are you here by yourself? Are you lost? What's in your bag?" I asked her, still sprawled on the tiles. What the hell was the Headshop doing, selling paraphernalia to a retard?

The Mall security jerk came over to see why I was talking to a chubby mental girl happily lying on the floor. "Move along ladies," he said, while smoothing his bushy mustache with his pointer finger. "Move along".

I grabbed Julie's hands and dragged her into a sitting position.

"My boyfriend is coming," said Julie. "We're going to meet the kittens at Pet Town. Want to come too?"

"Thanks but I'm meeting my friend in a few minutes."

"The kittens are so cute and I bet you want to marry my boyfriend."

What the hell was she talking about? What went on in that puffy red head?

"All the ladies love me," said a voice behind me.

I turned and it was Rob, shorter that I expected, but Rob.

"I'm Karen. Are you Julie's boyfriend?" I stammered.

"That's her version, not mine. We work together." Rob pushed his long hair behind his ear, a sliver of pink flashed from the cuff of his jean jacket.

"I think I've seen you at Work, Inc. Your name is Rob, right?"

"Yeah. The only way I can get out of the house is if I take Julie with me – she's my 200 pound watchdog and she's my sister."

This made no sense but maybe it did in a weird way.

"But you guys look nothing alike."

"Kittens! Kittens!" wailed Julie, collapsing back on the floor.

"Christ, shut up Julie!" Rob yelled. To me he said, "We don't look alike because we have different fathers. Our mom was a boozer and a groupie so our dads could be almost anybody with a warm van and all her drinking really fucked us up. That's why she's a retard and I have these." He flapped the wrists of his jean jacket. "They're the first thing everyone wants to know about so now the mystery is over. I've got it worse than Julie because at least I know I'm doomed but she has no clue that she's a freak."

"Come up to my office," Rob commanded and started walking to the door marked GARAGE STAIRS at the end of the hallway near the telephones. He walked without turning as if he knew that I would be right behind him.

I followed, leaving Julie crying and drooling on the Mall's checkerboard floor. Suddenly I didn't care if she was molested in the bathroom or kidnapped for medical testing. Suddenly Julie became disposable.

He led me to the top level of the parking garage and we sat on the steps, leaning against the rough cement walls. The town looked flat and grey from so high up and far away. I tried to figure out why I lived there, why anybody did.

"My dad, or the guy who thinks he is my dad, is Gus from Gus AllBrands Vacuums. When my Mom took off we started to live in the back of the shop. He thought she might come back if she knew where to find us. It's been seven years. There's no kitchen or real beds back there – just a tv and a hot plate. I've slept on lawn furniture since I was in junior high."

Rob wasn't embarrassed or mad; he was very matter-of-fact. It was just the way it was. I remembered walking by All Brands a few times, a sad store with a year round display of dirty snowblowers chained together outside.

Once a guy wearing a blue jumpsuit and an orange hat was leaning against the doorway with a can of cheap beer.

"Get out the bottle from my pocket," Rob instructed, and twisted, and offered me his side. I stuck my hand in his pocket, feeling sharp keys, a lighter, maybe a purse–size Visine, a linty lifesaver. I pulled out the bottle. It had its own little plastic cup on top. Nyquil.

"We eat a lot of cup-a-soup and cereal and sometimes toast cooked in Julie's easy bake oven. The hard part is making the bread tiny enough to fit through the door. Julie folds it up and it's like eating origami."

I opened the bottle and thought about the swan toast and pressed the bottle to his lips and he guzzled most of it, watching me. I drank the last sickly sweet sip and kissed him. His lips were slippery and when he smiled a single blue drop slid from the corner of his mouth.

"Okay, it's your turn," Rob said.

"What do you mean?" I asked, wiping my lips on the back of my hand.

"Now it's your turn," he repeated. "What are going to do for me?"

I shook my head. My mouth tasted like medicine.

"Let me decide for you," he said.

Rob pushed my head down with one hand and I closed my eyes and I bent over and he was pushing his hand into my mouth and I could taste him and the denim scratched my cheek and I sucked and pulled on the little fingers that weren't, trying to make them grow, to stretch them like a starfish, and I knew then, in that perfect moment, that I would never comb Rob's hair and feed him Doritos – I would be lighting his cigarettes and forging his disability checks – I would be his hands – and I knew then, as I was tracing the little nubs with my tongue, that I would never be happy.

FANTA

THE SUMMER I WAS 13, I was taking the bus to the town pool. It was dizzyingly, almost dazzlingly hot and bright, like I was living on the surface of the sun. That was the summer my second bestfriend Lance was trying to get me to trip with him. He was heavily into mushrooms. Lance had been trying to convince me for weeks. I refused. I think it was because I was a control freak and the whole experience seemed so, well, so vague. Logical as he was,

Lance gave me a greasy Carlos Castenada paperback to read so I could kind of understand what he was enjoying.

I hated to admit but it was fascinating – the lights, the colors, the fingerpainted dreamworld. I decided to see if I could achieve the same sensations by amateur means and started to experiment. Hanging upside down while holding my breath, rolling down hills blindfolded; I'd clamp my eyes shut and wait quietly for the fireworks.

Of course, my homemade headrushes could never measure up to the elaborate primordial stories from Castenada or Lance's slow motion revelations.

On the hottest summer day ever, I'm wearing white terrycloth shorts, a rainbow tank top and bluejean Dr. Scholls, and sitting on the curb waiting for the bus. Junky plastic sunglasses are clamped to my head. Next to me is a cheap drawstring bag filled with an Agatha Christie mystery, a too-small towel and a half-frozen can of orange Fanta soda.

My watch ticked loudly and as it got hotter, the ticking seemed even louder, like a bomb in a cartoon. I pushed my thumb really hard into my arm and held it there, trying to make ghost fingerprints, white against the reddened skin.

The heat, the ticktockticktock, the heaviness of my head – all I could think about was that Fanta.

I struggled with the poptop, slipping my finger under the thin aluminum disc, I flipped it and sucked the orange off my finger. The first sip was like drinking the only soda left in the world. The ice cold liquid, the fake sweetness, the microscopic bubbles coating my tongue and teeth.

Suddenly I felt a whisper, a miniature caress, the tiniest of movements in my shorts, a pulsating life force. I felt the infinite galaxies alive, swirling, the milky way threaded through the sparkling blackness. I felt the pulsating energy of the planets, the stars, the suns; the promise of worlds unexplored.

I opened my eyes and looked down to see ants tracing the edges of my terrycloth shorts, like a fabric highway, and disappear beneath the stretched out elastic of my flowered underwear.

My desperate teenage daydream for my very own outergalactic experience, mindblowing, heartracing, chest pounding and everything else, had been reduced to an anthill in Connecticut. These intruders, aliens, uninvited and crawling inside me, on me, my crevices have become their personal planet.

Hundreds, thousands, even millions of them, ants, silent explorers, marching through my body, up all its trails and branches and rivers, in single file, to slowly disappear as their routes lead to nowhere.

HAIRCUT

ALL THAT SUMMER I worked the 5pm-1am shift at Friendly's – backwards from the rest of the world or at least the rest of the kids in my high school. Then I'd sleep until noon, swim a few laps in our pool, and doze on a lawn chair, the crossword puzzle book tenting my face. Once I woke up to my mother clipping my bangs: "The only time you do what I tell you to do," she laughed. I wore a headband for weeks.

I loved being a waitress. I was fast, funny, and efficient. I wore the shortest and tightest uniform I could zip myself into and left every night with my polyester pockets bulging with soggy bills and silver quarters.

There was a predictable rhythm to the nights. First came the supper crowds of awkward first daters and young families with whining kids. Then the restaurant emptied, like the tide rushing out, and us girls mopped up puddles of chocolate milk, sorted silverware, drank TAB out of coffee cups and smoked shitty menthol cigarettes. Soon the second wave began, whooshing in drunk teenagers, tired traveling salesman and pairs of chain smoking airplane pilots. They always wore their uniforms and were the best tippers.

Each week was a litany of missing French fries, ripped nylons and bickering bus boys, punctuated by pockets of excitement – the cops arresting an escaped fugitive in the men's room; a busload of professional wrestlers stranded with two flat tires and signing autographs in the non-smoking section until the tow truck showed up. And once Chris swore he saw Evel Knievel ordering a chocolate chip cone at the take out window.

Around 1:30 after the stragglers were finally kicked out and the booths had a last wipe down, everyone headed home and I headed to Peter's house. Peter was my friend the insomniac who lived halfway between the restaurant and my house. He left a flashlight in the mailbox for me to use to find my way to his tent in the backyard.

Peter had planned to go to astronomy summer school in Arizona, but a week before he attempted to make hash brownies in his little sister's Easy Bake Oven and burned down the garage. His parents cancelled the trip. So Peter vowed to recreate his missed adventure and pitched a tent in his backyard. He cut a hole in the roof of the tent for his telescope to watch the night sky and his little sister dragged out a cooler and her Girl Scout sleeping bag for him. It was perfect. He read and mowed lawns all day, ate cereal for every meal and then got out his notebooks and telescope each night to see the stars.

My entrance fee was a drooping butterscotch sundae that I made especially for him before I ended my shift. We'd sit in lawn chairs in the dark, Peter shirtless and in his dungarees shorts and me barefoot in my waitress uniform. The grass was cold and green and the yard was very quiet. Peter would slowly eat his sundae clockwise and I would smoke and watch the spirals float away from my face and disappear into the world. We didn't really talk that much.

Peter's astronomy notebooks were filled with rows of numbers and drawings and the names of constellations that sounded like secret spells – Cassiopeia, Corvus, Cygnus, Equuleus. If the night was super crisp and clear, we would open up the sleeping bag and Peter would point out the constellations to me, sometimes taking my hand to trace them out in the sky. Those were the only stars I still remembered years later.

Some nights we would just hang out in the tent and roll up all of my waitress change. Peter kept a coffee can filled with empty paper rolls and I separated my coins into little piles and he would fill the tiny paper tubes and stack them up like miniature Lincoln logs. We listened to his small transistor radio while we worked, mostly to the crazy talk radio stations; chatty divorcees discussing their alien abductions and paranoid old bachelors confiding their plans to booby trap their houses to keep the IRS agents away. One of us would laugh randomly.

The traffic on the interstate grew louder around 3am – tractor trailer trucks mostly – and I would grab my stuff and drive home and crawl into bed. Nobody knew about our nightly visits and even the two of us couldn't remember how they began. I had been inside the house only once but the dolls scared me. Peter's mother collected dolls and the living room became her display area. There were big dolls and small dolls, dolls holding the tiny flags of their native lands, orphaned dolls adopted from the bins of the Salvation Army, dolls rescued from the sticky hands of ungrateful toddlers, and dolls that were last minute purchases from airport duty free shops. Hundreds of dolls, all horrible. The first and only time I walked through the room I felt like millions of dead eyes were following me, all those frozen hands reaching out, as if they were all Peter's mother trying to protect her son in the darkness. That was when Peter started leaving the flashlight out for me.

On the very last night of the summer it was so hot Peter's butterscotch sundae melted into a yellowy soup before I even reached his house. I found him setting up our lawn chairs in the path of the lawn sprinkler. We both plopped into the seats, scrunching our faces as the water smashed into us, on cue, every 30 seconds, as the sprinkler spun and sputtered in its noisy circle. After 10 minutes of this, my uniform became wet and stiff like a suit of armor, and I begged Peter for a Tshirt to change into. He rummaged for his in the tent and when he handed it to me it was still warm, like his skin. He unzipped my long zipper and I stepped out of my uniform, leaving it like a soggy tube on the grass and pulled the Tshirt over my head.

"You look like a hippie," I said to him. "When did your hair get so long?"

Peter tucked a wet handful of blonde hair behind his ear. "It just happens. And school starts next week. Will you cut it for me?"

"I have no idea what I'm doing but I'll try. Can you find some scissors?"

He dragged one lawn chair onto a dry spot on the grass and went into the door of the kitchen. His white back reflected the light from the kitchen ceiling as he flicked on the switch, a bright flash I could see across the backyard. Peter came out with a comb and some orange handled kid's scissors. "Sorry but these are all I could find – my little sister's craft scissors. They kind of suck but do the best you can."

Peter sat in the chair. "Can you see?"

"Not really. I can give you a Braille haircut."

"Wait a second," Peter said, as he rummaged around the lawn for a few minutes and came back triumphantly with the flashlight. "Here", he said as he sat back down and shined the flashlight under his chin.

The flashlight reflected concentric circles of light and shadow around Peter's head. The scissors were meant for construction paper, not hair, and I had to slowly saw away at small chunks a little at a time. The hair fell and drifted and stuck to Peter's damp shoulders like a furry cape. I absently tried to sweep some off but it was hopeless.

I felt something strange and soft and insistent brushing against my cheek and looked up to small blurs of white buzzing around. Dozens of moths were surrounding us, swooping into the flashlight's beam.

"This is impossible. The moths are flying into my face and making me crazy. Shut off the flashlight before I swallow one."

Peter clicked off the switch and it took a few seconds for my eyes to adjust to the blackness that soon became grey. We were both quiet and still as we watched the stars in the sky and the fireflies that were like miniature stars hover and dart through the bushes. "Look there, that constellation is Andromeda," Peter said, as he took my hand and pointed. "See? Andromeda is one of my favorites. A king was told to chain his daughter to a rock to sacrifice her to a sea monster and save his kingdom. But she was rescued by Perseus and they had 6 daughters."

I could see the chains of stars above us and I could see Andromeda in my mind, chained to that rock. "I can do this," I told Peter. "I don't need the light." And I gently spread out my fingers onto his head like a fan and used them as my guides, as I slowly cut away at his hair, on the last day of summer.

AIR

IT WAS A SUMMER OF NO PARENTS and a stolen copy of the *Guinness Book of World Records*. We all became obsessed with getting into the book. Obviously there were some things we automatically couldn't do like own the world's biggest diamond or drive the fastest race car ever. I often wondered how the lady with the world's longest fingernails brushed her teeth and why the oldest mother decided to have a baby at 91.

But that still left a pretty good list of the records we could waste all summer vacation trying to beat. Linda fell down the stairs while jumping rope for 2 hours, 46 minutes and 15 seconds, and Robby passed out attempting to hold his breathe underwater, floating up to the water's surface in slow motion. All of us were grounded for the weekend after that one.

Sometimes Todd, on his way home from bagging groceries at A&P, would ride his bike onto my front lawn and ask about our daily record-breaking activities. "Any fatalities today?" Was his favorite question, as he pulled at his sweat sticky shirt, making wet pyramids spring up on his chest, his stomach.

"Have you ever heard of Harry Houdini, the greatest magician in the world?" Suddenly he pulled off his polyester work shirt and wrapped it around his head like a turban. "If you could beat one of his records, you would definitely get into the Book. It would be a fucking cinch."

And then he jumped on his bike, slowly sinking into the wet grass, leaving a snail trail to the curb.

• • •

THE FIRST TIME Todd swore he would bury me alive I pretended I didn't hear him.

Todd's parents were divorced and he lived with his father, Gary. Gary had a bushy mustache and wore necklaces and looked like Burt Reynolds. He had a waterbed that we all heard endlessly about. Us girls wondered if we would get seasick or dizzy or both. And he insisted we call him Gary, which we all agreed was just messed up. I mean, he was still an adult, even if he was the most unadult adult we knew.

At the end of our street was a small path in the woods that led to the golf course. Susan and Melanie and I spent lost hours there, sunning on the too-short benches, our knees bent like triangles. We sifted through the sand traps for soda money dropped by clumsy golfers, mostly our dads.

On a boring Tuesday, after too many episodes of Police Woman, I followed Todd up the path. He ditched his bike near the giant mountain laurel bush and changed direction, walking away from the golf course and up a steep hill.

I kept my distance but of course he knew I was there – he had to. I sneezed, I tripped over branches, I coughed down a mosquito. And still Todd kept walking, almost running, until he reached a weird rocky section, as if someone had cut off a chunk of the moon and plopped it into the middle of Connecticut. Todd spun around and I pathetically hid behind a tiny tree.

He shook his head. "Wow – if we were in Vietnam, you would be dead already. You sound like a bowling ball rolling through those fucking trees."

Still behind the tree, I said, " I know. It looks so much easier on tv."

"Come on out," said Todd. "We have a lot to do. I've been preparing. We're going to be famous. You're going to get into the *Guinness Book of World Records*." He absentmindedly rubbed his wispy mustache.

I pulled a spider out of my hair. "No way will I eat live goldfish. Anything snake related is okay. Tarantulas-probably not. I get sick on roller coasters and I doubt my mother will let me go to Antarctica."

"None of those things matter. I am going to bury you alive."

I scratched my shin and adjusted my sock. "I doubt my mother will let me leave the country. We usually eat dinner at 6 o' clock."

"I told you about Houdini before. So this will be Houdini but better. We can practice every day to build up your lungs and then, when you're ready, we can make it official, on the record. My uncle is a notary. He will sign the paperwork for us and then mail it in."

My stomach was churning. "I'm not sure I can do this. I think I need to leave."

Todd shook his head. "You can do it, but you just don't realize it yet. Meet me back here tomorrow so we can start training."

"Goodbye!" he yelled at my back as I ran past him down the hill.

···

I DID SHOW UP in the woods the next day. I'm still not sure why. I was scared of Todd but I couldn't seem to say no to him. It was like eating a carton of malted milk balls. I knew they would make me sick – they always did – but I would gobble down every last one, the satisfying crunch and chalky taste of each ball exploding in my mouth like a soon-to-be nauseating firework.

Not knowing what supplies we would need to break the world record, I filled my backpack with stuff I could steal that wouldn't be missed – a flashlight, potato chips, pillows, the TV guide, and extra socks. I figured Todd would bring the technical stuff.

Todd was already at the site when I got there, unloading his duffel bag – a miniature shovel, egg timer, canteen, sleeping bag, bathing cap and a snorkel. He was wearing a too heavy sweatshirt and seemed hot and kind of nervous.

"I think I am ready for this," I said. "What do I need to do? They better spell my name right in the Guinness Book!"

"We can do this if we work together, " Todd promised. "I brought my notes. I have a plan, a step by step plan."

"Good. I need a system – it makes me feel better," I said.

"Step 1," said Todd, reading from his tiny spiral notebook, "dig a hole." He held up a tiny camping shovel – actually it was more like a trowel.

"That thing? A hole will take forever with that thing." He started to dig. I sat on a stump and attempted the *TV Guide* crossword puzzle. I read the clues out loud and Todd grunted out the answers between trowel loads of dirt and sticks and pine needles.

"4-down. 8 letters. Son-in-law from 'All in the Family'.

"Meathead."

"Correct. 6-down. 6 letters. Popular sitcom. 'Welcome Back blank'.

"Kotter."

"Correct."

We worked our way through the puzzle and ate some chips and after about an hour, the hole looked like a second grader might fit in it.

"I need to leave to eat supper – dinner time is my curfew," I said, offering myself an escape and I left. As I walked home I began to realize that with an obviously unexperienced guy like Todd in charge, this world record might not happen.

The next afternoon I came back to find Todd filthy and sitting on a big mound of dirt piled next to a surprisingly big-enough, completely dug out hole. Maybe Todd was more motivated that I thought.

"Lay down next to it so we can see if it's long enough."

I did and we measured.

Step 1 was complete.

Todd read from his tiny spiral notebook. "Step 2 – practice runs. Practice is very important because it prepares us for anything that could happen. Surprises are not good when you are training for a world record."

He dramatically unrolled the sleeping bag. "This will be your base of operations. You need to practice and work up your endurance. First thing is getting used to being in a small space for a long time."

Todd spread out the sleeping bag in the damp hole and unzipped the flap. I grabbed my pillow and shimmied in. Todd zipped the zipper all the way to my chin. "This isn't so bad," I said.

"All the way in," Todd said. "Your head too. That's why I brought the snorkel for you to use." He pushed it into the sleeping bag and I fumbled with the plastic mouthpiece. It felt like I was wearing someone else's retainer, way too big and bulky and awkward. It was impossible to breathe. I pulled it out. "I can't do this. It's not right. I feel like I'm choking."

Todd looked concerned. "Maybe it's too much all at once. Get used to breathing through the snorkel first and we can add the sleeping bag later." He patted a tree stump. "Sit here and put on the mask and read a magazine for a while. Practice your breathing and just relax."

I sat and again wedged in the hard plastic mouthpiece. It was still awkward but I felt more in control sitting up, rather than zipped into, the sleeping bag. After a while, my mouth relaxed around it. I started to focus on my breathing. Breathing was a weird thing to think about. It just happened automatically, like blinking or walking, and when you tried to take it apart, to dissect how it happened, it wrecked the whole process. I felt like an alien learning how to live on earth. Breathe in, hold it, breathe out. Breathe in, hold it, breathe out.

When it got easier, I read the magazine for a while. Todd seemed happy. "You seem so much better. Let's add the eye mask now," he said, handing me the rest of the snorkel set. "When you're finally buried, you'll need this to protect your eyes."

He stretched the thick rubber band of the mask over my head, tucking it behind my ears: the left, the right. He licked his palm and smoothed down my hair. "You look a little crazy sitting there, wearing the snorkel and reading a magazine. But speaking as your trainer, it all totally makes sense. We are going to break the record."

I was enjoying the article "Lipstick Versus Lipgloss" when my goggles started to fog up. Todd sighed. "It's all about learning to breathe a new way. And then we need to build on that. Why don't we quit for the day and you wear the snorkel on the way home to practice? And maybe you can do some extra credit homework and wear the snorkel around your house. The more practice time, the better."

"Ok," I said, as I headed home, wiping the fog from my goggles with my fingertips, like tiny windshield wipers. I tripped over a few branches as I walked down the path. I was starting to understand how the Olympic athletes felt, always training and always hopeful about their world records.

That night after dinner, I took a shower, pulled on my nightgown and the snorkel, and went down to the living room to watch tv. My father was, as usual, in his chair, with the remote control in one hand and an exploded bag of potato chips in his lap.

"What the hell is on your head?" he asked me.

I sighed. "I'm, uh, practicing for a school project."

"It's summer. There is no school."

"This is extra credit for next year."

He shook his head, potato chip crumbs flying. "At least you aren't shoplifting and getting into trouble like all the other kids."

I laughed. "No, I'm studying."

"As long as the cops aren't knocking on my door, I don't care what you're doing." He fumbled with the remote. "What channel is our program on?"

"Three."

And with me in my snorkel and Dad crunching his bag of chips, we watched *Columbo.*

• • •

I BEGAN TO SPEND the afternoons at Todd's house, when his shift at the A&P was done. It was way too hot outside at the golf course and since Gary was the King of the AC, their house was like Alaska. The dark walls and shag carpeting and leather couches had a weird Flintstones feeling.

I saw my very first avocado in Gary and Todd's kitchen. I remember that avocado because it seemed so cool, so sophisticated, so Cosmopolitan Magazine, when the rest of us lived on bologna sandwiches and bruised bananas. But then we all had mothers instead of avocados.

Todd smuggled me Lifesavers from the supermarket and I helped him figure out how to use the washing machine. He finally shaved his wispy mustache and suddenly seemed much cuter. While I was plopped in one of the dangerously gigantic bean bag chairs and practicing with the snorkel, Todd read versions of his trainer's speech, written on the back of old recipe cards. He said he wanted to sound prepared but natural when he was interviewed on tv.

"Today we need to move to Step 3-isolation." Todd rummaged around in the hall closet and dragged out the tootsie roll of a sleeping bag. He untied the ties, jerked it into the air, and let it float to the floor.

"Let's try this again, he said, as he unzipped the noisy metal zipper. I adjusted the snorkel and wriggled inside. When I was completely in, I nodded to Todd and he zipped me up tightly, the snorkel poking out like a periscope.

Slowly my eyes adjusted to the darkness. Instead of brightness and shapes, there was just levels of blackness, from grey to black to the very darkest I could imagine. Sounds from the outside world were muffled and I could hear my heart beating loudly, too loudly, in my ears, a cartoon heart from Saturday mornings.

I felt like I was nowhere and everywhere at the same time. I thought of that science class movie about cells and equilibrium – for the cell to be balanced and stay alive, there needs to be a constant recalibration between the inside and the outside of the cell, a fluidity. And in this weird and dark and undistracted space, my insides were emanating out but there was nothing outside to go back in to replace them. I was emptying.

Suddenly a very heavy weight lowered itself onto me. "Are you okay in there?" Todd shouted through the sleeping bag, towards my face. His feet were tucked under mine, his palms at my waist, as if he was doing push-ups.

I nodded yes through the thick fabric. Todd relaxed and I could feel him sinking onto me even more, the sleeping bag outlining my edges. It was getting warmer and I felt fuzzy and my breathing started to shift.

The encyclopedia (Volume H, Human Body, Respiration) explained that the average person can easily hold her breath for 30 seconds, but can be trained to last much longer. However, the hardest thing to learn is to ignore the mind and the body's compulsion to breathe, to understand that the body can function with the oxygen it already has. To be in control while letting go.

"I think I need to kiss you," yelled Todd and his hands surrounded where he thought my face would be in the sleeping bag, pressing his mouth to where mine might be. I could only taste the two barriers – cotton and plastic.

Suddenly, the arc of the zipper unzipped, and the blinding darkness became a blinding brightness, and I squeezed my eyes together even tighter for protection. Todd's fingers gently opened my lips and removed the bulky plastic. I could still feel the ghost of the mouthpiece as Todd kissed me, like there were two mouths on mine.

I opened my eyes and looked into Todd's. He seemed panicked. "What if this violates some international rule of conduct? After all our training – we could be disqualified!"

"Only if someone finds out," I said, "and no one here is going to squeal. I know I'm not. Are you?"

"Of course not."

"Then stop worrying. And anyway, my mouth feels out of order. Let's take a break and have an avocado sandwich."

. . .

My TRAINING became slower and harder. We both realized I had to wean myself off the snorkel and rely on my own ability to hold my breath. And I had to ignore the panic in my brain and my body when they started to fight for air even though there was plenty of oxygen in me. And way too many afternoons were spent making out at Todd's house, once even on Gary's waterbed (yes, it was like kissing on the Titanic after it hit the iceberg). But we did get through the training schedule and with each practice I built up another few seconds endurance. I finally reached 3 minutes and 21 seconds.

On Sunday, Todd stole Gary's Polaroid camera and we walked hand in hand past the golf course, through the woods and to the World Record set up. The sleeping bag was neatly laid out in the hole and next to it was a lawn chair. A small shovel leaned against a tree.

Very carefully Todd laid out the supplies next to the hole – flashlight, goggles, stop watch, a can of Tab and the Polaroid camera.

"I think we should start at 12 sharp – it seems more official" said Todd, and I agreed. I bent my head and Todd stretched and adjusted the goggles over my eyes, carefully tucking my hair under the strap. Then I grabbed the flashlight and stepped down into hole. The triangle of the sleeping bag was flipped open, like a bed in a hotel, and I wriggled inside.

I wasn't sure where to put my hands – I guess I never really thought that part out – so I left them resting at my sides; the flashlight was cold and metallic against my leg. The Polaroid "Popped!" "Clicked!" "Shhhh-ed!" as the wet tongue of film ejected from the camera. Todd flapped the sticky print in the air for a few seconds before he wrote "11:50" on its white border. The documentation had begun.

Todd grabbed the shovel and began to throw dirt into the hole and onto the sleeping bag. I quietly watched through the goggles as the pile of dirt got smaller and the weight on top of me became heavier. It felt like someone was throwing phone books on me. This was different than being buried at the beach. This dirt was darker, heavier, wetter, somehow more sinister.

When the thick layer of dirt started to press the fabric onto and around me, it was time to zip up the sleeping bag and start the stop watch for the World Record and continue the burial. As Todd finally pulled the sleeping bag zipper closed, his face slowly vanished as the metal teeth locked together, shutting me inside the darkness, like a bank vault door slamming.

"12:00".

Todd kept shoveling, the dirt molding the sleeping bag around me, my body, my face, like a prison of earth, a second skin. The sheer weight of the dirt pushing down on me, pushing me back into the earth itself, was making me panic. This relentless pressure was new and terrifying; it had never come up in our practice sessions. My breathe was trapped. I struggled to open my mouth but my lips were like cement. I understood this is what it is to be dead. An enveloping blackness. A pushing out of life, like a foot stepping on a balloon.

I was drowning without water.

"12:03!" I faintly heard from a voice that seemed very small and far away.

The dark weight pressed down on me, heavier. The air in my body felt stuck inside me, trapped, and I tried to inhale a new breathe, but there was no room. My legs and arms twitched and kicked deep in a silent karate fight. I had to get out.

"No! Not yet! Just another 2 minutes!" Todd yelled.

Thrashing inside the sleeping bag, I could feel the heavy dirt slowly cracking around me, like little earthquakes. Gasping I tried to gulp down air that was not here.

"Don't ruin this for me!"

I could feel his words falling on me, each as heavy as a shovelful of dirt. And at last, I pushed and rose up in the filthy sleeping bag crypt, my shaking hands searching for the zipper and yanking it down and swallowing the fresh air in greedy mouthfuls like a fish thrown onto the shore. And above me the sky was flat and blinding and the most beautiful blue I had ever seen.

About the Author

Lauren Leja is a writer, photographer, snapshot collector and rescuer of the forgotten. She has a website, invisiblecommute.com, in which she documents her wanderings with a daily photo. Lauren lives in Boston.

Nixes Mate Books features small-batch artisanal literature, created by writers that use all 26 letters of the alphabet and then some, honing their craft the time-honored way: one line at a time.

More Nixes Mate titles:
On Broad Sound | Rusty Barnes
Kinky Keeps the House Clean | Mari Deweese
Squall Line on the Horizon | Pris Campbell
Comes to This | Jeff Weddle
Hitchhiking Beatitudes | Michael McInnis

Forthcoming titles from Nixes Mate:
Waiting for an Answer | Heather Sullivan
Nixes Mate Review Anthology 2016/17
Capp Road | Matt Borczon
A World Where | Paul Brookes
Lubbock Electric | Anne Elezabeth Pluto
A Southern Childhood | Pris Campbell
Secret Histories | Michael McInnis

nixesmate.pub/books

Made in the USA
Middletown, DE
20 June 2017